EPIC ADVENTURES

Edited By Megan Roberts

First published in Great Britain in 2020 by:

Young Writers
Remus House
Coltsfoot Drive
Peterborough
PE2 9BF
Telephone: 01733 890066
Website: www.youngwriters.co.uk

Printed and bound in the UK by BookPrintingUK
Website: www.bookprintinguk.com
YB0436B

FOREWORD

Welcome, Reader!

Are you ready to enter the Adventure Zone? Then come right this way - your portal to endless new worlds awaits. It's very simple, all you have to do is turn the page and you'll be transported into a wealth of super stories.

Is it magic? Is it a trick? No! It's all down to the skill and imagination of primary school pupils from around the country. We gave them the task of writing a story on any topic, and to do it in just 100 words! I think you'll agree they've achieved that brilliantly – this book is jam-packed with exciting and thrilling tales.

These young authors have brought their ideas to life using only their words. This is the power of creativity and it gives us life too! Here at Young Writers we want to pass our love of the written word onto the next generation and what better way to do that than to celebrate their writing by publishing it in a book!

It sets their work free from homework books and notepads and puts it where it deserves to be – out in the world and preserved forever. Each awesome author in this book should be **super proud** of themselves, and now they've got proof of their ideas and their creativity in black and white, to look back on in years to come!

We hope you enjoy this book as much as we have. Now it's time to let imagination take control, so read on...

CONTENTS

Hundon Community Primary School, Hundon

Bebe Scarlett Lansdown (10)	47
Amy Harper (10)	48
Niamh Mitson (9)	49
Finley Simpson (10)	50
George Speller (9)	51
Lola-Rose Slater (10)	52
Thomas Jeggo (11)	53
Grace Daniels (10)	54
Marisol Brown (9)	55
Riley George Morgan-Jones (9)	56
Harvey Richardson-Capoling (10)	57
Erin May Jeggo (9)	58
Grae Mileham (11)	59
Harper George Porter Tabrar (9)	60
Alex Sharpe (10)	61
Amelie Sullivan (10)	62
Gabriel Parker-Hall (9)	63
Perdita Maisie Jones (11)	64

London Meed CP School, Burgess Hill

Nakshatra Manasani (10)	65
Imogen Porter (11)	66
Verity Collins (11)	67
Archie Townsend (11)	68
Leo Rimmer (11)	69
Grace Lily Chambers (10)	70
Sophie Stacey (11)	71
Phoebe Brown (10)	72

Millway Primary School, Duston

Taha Karegar (8)	73
Eloise Baker (8)	74
Jasmyn-Rae McDonald (8)	75
Edmund Puchovic (8)	76
Oliwier Gronski (8)	77
Peaches-Blossom June Gooding (9)	78
Lucas Smith (8)	79

Normanton House School, Derby

Aminah Khan (9)	80
Eshaal Shahzad (9)	81
Naafi Bin Naeem (9)	82
Zahra Sohail (7)	83

Roe Green Junior School, Kingsbury

Usmaan Parvez (9)	84
Rupin Bakrania (8)	85
Preet Pravin Hirani (9)	86
Chahat Piyushbhai Patel (9)	87
Neya Patel (7)	88
Safiyah Uddin (9)	89
Alexandra Bosnea (7)	90
Saiswin Thusyanthan (7)	91
Stefania Antonesi (8)	92
Darius Bobieca (9)	93
Sara Maria Ungureanu (8)	94
Samuel Horandau (7)	95
Riyaan Adams (8)	96
Nandika Agarwal (9)	97
Ifeoluwa Coker (11)	98
Sami Raza (7)	99
Kiya Gami (7)	100
Aruvi Niranjan (9)	101
Hadiya Habib (7)	102
Abdul Rasheed Ahmed (9)	103
Laiqah Batool (10)	104
Iman Ahmed (8)	105
Prem Dave (10)	106
Monisha Kerai (9)	107
Hasan Mohamed Rizath (9)	108
Reiko McDonald (8)	109
Janice Wong (7)	110
David Bordei (7)	111
Ghulam Mustafa (9)	112

St Cuthbert's Primary School, Glasgow

Coco Kexin He (7)	113
Elizabeth (6)	114
Yostina Yemane (7)	115
Joshua Wilson Albert (7)	116
Jenna Chi (8)	117
Poppy Kelly (7)	118
Tyler Redmond (7)	119
Zoey Guan (7)	120
April Newton Green (7)	121
Patience Asemota (7)	122

Tany's Dell Primary School & Nursery, Harlow

Maya Mohamed (11)	123
Harrison Houghton (11)	124
Lara Burke (10)	125
Laura Lakatosova (10)	126
Perla Grigalaityte (11)	127
Tegan Rose Roberts (11)	128
Jack Stone (10)	129
Alfie Chivrall (11)	130
Caitlin Moriarty (10)	131
Iisha-Lemay Myers (10)	132
Kacper Zapior (10)	133
Teddy Cleverdon (10)	134
Jake Carter (10)	135
Nicolas Gecmen (10)	136
Oliver Quinn (10)	137
Isabelle Walker (11)	138
Archie Perks (11)	139
Oliver Berger (10)	140
Cameron Bullock (11)	141
Alfie Hopkins (11)	142
Archie Cleall (10)	143
Niall Wright (10)	144
Ronnie Wood (10)	145
Siobhan David (10)	146
Lily-May Morton (10)	147
Chloe Browne (10)	148
Mikel Appleton (11)	149

Liam Willis (11)	150
Max Peter Allen (11)	151
James Forrest (11)	152
Rosie Barker (11)	153
Brendon Dakin (10)	154
Gabriella Gora (10)	155
Owen Ellis Halls (10)	156
Kamil Zapior (10)	157
Jayden O'Reilly (10)	158
Tegan Elizabeth Hodgson (10)	159
Una Venezia Turner-Porter (10)	160

The Forest School, Knaresborough

Albert Lock (10)	161
Jack	162
Nieve Mountford (10)	163
Leo Hill (10)	164
William Whitehead	165
Sophie	166
Conner	167

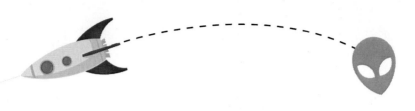

THE STORIES

TOP SECRET

Shape-Shifting School

As night fell, the shape-shifters were unleashed and the portal laughed diabolically. I stepped in, I could feel the spirits enveloping me.

When I was there, I caught something from the corner of my eye. It looked demonic, but then it started to change its shape. I decided to walk the other way. While I was walking up the stairs, a door slammed behind me. I could see a shadow getting closer as I was running up the stairs. Suddenly, I had a feeling of regret. I ran into a classroom and waited in it. The thing stared at me...

Alba Rae Williams (9)
Aberdare Park Primary School, Trecynon

The House

He walked in, looking for a missing person. He couldn't find them anywhere. He looked through the whole country. He examined the picture closely. Little did he know, he had amnesia.

His memories came rushing back to him, he was the missing person! He searched for answers for who he was. He lived two lives and had the same career. He went back to a normal life. He found his family, his parents were glad they'd found him. They bonded. The house he'd searched for was his old family home. They all lived happily ever after.

Zac Floyd (9)
Aberdare Park Primary School, Trecynon

The Magic Portal

One day, my friend Courey and I, Connor, went up the country park for a walk. We were walking under a large tree. Suddenly, a mist appeared in front of us. We walked through...
We were transported to a mysterious future. The first thing we saw was a girl flying on a floating fossil, but then I saw dinosaurs surrounding us! Would they want to play or attack? We didn't want to stay long enough to find out! We decided to run back through the mist in case it disappeared and we would be stuck in the future forever...

Connor Jeffrey Martin (10)
Aberdare Park Primary School, Trecynon

The Missing Bigfoot

Bigfoot had escaped. Detectives were trying to find him. They found Bigfoot but he didn't look right. The detective saw that it was a mask, so they took it off. It revealed the person under the mask and they found out that it was an escaped prisoner! They put him back in jail and they found a load of Bigfoot's hair. They followed the trail of hair and found Bigfoot! They decided to leave him alone because he hadn't done anything wrong, so they decided to let Bigfoot be free.

Tegan Jonathan (10)
Aberdare Park Primary School, Trecynon

Being A Cat For A Day

As I slept, a group of witches passed my window. They cast a spell on me...

In the morning, I woke up in a cat's body! Then, my mum came in. She grabbed my cat that was in my body! Mum made her get dressed and go to school.

When I got up, I went to the garden to play with my ball, then a bird stole it! I chased him down the street. *Phew!* I got it back! Finally, it was time for bed. I thought, *I kinda like being a cat!* But, the next day, I was human...

Louisa Grace Mears (10)

Aberdare Park Primary School, Trecynon

The Surprise

Hi, my name is Colby. I have epilepsy. I get picked on a lot. Mac is my best friend, he is from my school. Two weeks ago, he left to go to Australia because his parents needed to work, that means I don't see him and I get picked on a lot more.
It's my birthday today, my mam has planned a surprise for me and she won't tell me what it is. We went to Australia! As soon as we got there, I knew why... To see Mac! We got to be best friends all over again!

Summer Ann Moore (10)
Aberdare Park Primary School, Trecynon

The Girl And The Wave

The wave was on its way. The wave got mad any time you talked badly about it, which my mates were doing! The wave jumped up and screamed! We screamed back in fear. The wave was crying and said, "I need friends!"
We said, "We will be your friends!" and then, before I knew it, we were in an underwater mansion and we were breathing fine! That was the happy ending of my journey!

Lily Evans (9)
Aberdare Park Primary School, Trecynon

The Land Of Mythical Creatures

Early in the morning, Dove went to the forest and listened to the birds singing. She always sang with the birds. While she was singing, suddenly, she heard a sound behind the bushes. She crept forward and she was brave enough to go and see what it was.

Dove saw a magical, pink, sparkly portal. She put her whole body through and went in. She saw so many mythical creatures like unicorns, goblins and monsters and much more!

A fairy said she was going to be the queen of the land. They all had a big feast. She was triumphant!

Areeba Noor (9)

Beech Hill Community Primary School, Luton

Me And Hydra, My Magical Dragon

As I woke up to go to school, all I could see was light shining on my face. I soon realised that it was a magical portal! I stepped into it and gazed at the new world. It was raining diamonds and dragonfruits were growing on trees! In the distance, I saw a glorious dragon beside a tall caste. I dashed towards it, then I was flying on it! A while later, I glanced at citizens walking their dragons and even unicorns! I couldn't believe what I was seeing but, unfortunately, time was running out. I soon went home...

Aishah Bint-Anwar (9)
Beech Hill Community Primary School, Luton

The Return

The Earth was evacuated hundreds of years ago due to a massive explosion. My first instinct drove me to escape space and come to Earth to see if it was safe for my people.

When I landed, it took me a few seconds to adjust myself to the vivid light of the beaming sun's rays and the smell of nature. I opened my eyes to a field of people bowing down to me, shouting, "Hail to the new commander of Earth!" The most powerful sense of confusion struck me when I noticed that I was sitting on a throne...

Rufaida Ahmed (10)
Beech Hill Community Primary School, Luton

Fairy Land Queen

In my dream, fast asleep, I stepped into a mythical forest. Not knowing what to do, I found a wooden door. I stepped inside and saw fairies and pixies and dragonflies. I was amazed until I felt like I wasn't on land... I closed my eyes and I moved my shoulders. My head felt weak... I was flying! I made new friends, fairies, pixies and dragonflies acted insanely strange then, all of a sudden, everyone bowed. I could see the beautiful trees, houses and everything, and I saw the queen of the magical land!

Samira Shara (9)
Beech Hill Community Primary School, Luton

Nightmare Horror!

As I stepped into the world of my own, out in the night, I was suddenly in a trance. I could see the black fires of Hell, the heat boiling me making me sweat. There stood a figure, a bloodthirsty man glancing at my daring, teal eyes. I could see him looking at me as his next victim. His trident was as red as blood. The scorching sun high above my sweaty skull, I could see deadly asteroids charging down like wrecking balls. This could only mean I was in Hell! How? It was my worst nightmare...

Talal Tariq (10)
Beech Hill Community Primary School, Luton

Magical Candy World...

I strolled forward, confused, when I gazed at the bright circle. It dragged me inside, not knowing it was a portal. I saw a pink sun and blue grass. The rocks were red and the clouds were purple. In the distance, I glanced at a palace decorated with candy. Beside the palace, I saw a magical unicorn. I walked there and rode on it and it was talking! I went into the palace and ate so much candy! But then suddenly, I saw a tunnel and something was shining. It was the same portal! I went home.

Malaika Rafiq (10)
Beech Hill Community Primary School, Luton

Dragon World

I stumbled upon this glistening portal, wondering what was behind it. When I went in, I stared up at the clouds and saw a whole family on a baby dragon as if they were birds in the sky. I was petrified when more baby dragons came out with their families. I stared at the pitch-black cave. I walked slowly and quietly. I saw a mother dragon just on the floor at the back of the cave. It woke up and asked me if I wanted a ride, so I got on and flew. That was the best day!

Abdul Qasim Miah (9)
Beech Hill Community Primary School, Luton

Picture Come To Life

I stepped through the bridge and immediately arrived somewhere else. I thought I recognised it because it was like the drawing I did an hour ago. I saw some people pooping in their pants and some going wild like animals. Quickly, I saw a snake man, but I was strong and I had a strong, dark sword! Snake Man's first attack was getting a snake to try and bite me but, I killed the snake as quick as a flash and then killed Snake Man for good!

Luqmaan Hussain (10)
Beech Hill Community Primary School, Luton

The Magical Unicorn

Once upon a time, there was a girl called Kes. She once went to a magical rainforest. She was looking for a unicorn. She was looking and looking for an injured unicorn to save. Then suddenly, a hopping unicorn came. The unicorn started to chase her. She was running and running but suddenly, a tree was in front of her! The unicorn jumped over it. She was really frightened but then Kes realised it went to give her a hug! The unicorn then stayed with Kes and Kes' mum and dad forever. She called the unicorn Miss Rainbow Crossley!

Kesania Crossley (8)
Christchurch Junior School, Christchurch

Superhero Unicorn And The Baddie

One day, there was a unicorn superhero. There was a baddie who wanted to destroy the unicorn's castle! So, Superhero Unicorn wanted to stop him from knocking the castle down. She had a sword and, good news, the baddie didn't have anything to protect himself apart from a knife to chop the castle down! When he was getting attacked by Superhero Unicorn, all he did was hit her back. Every time he did that, Superhero Unicorn said, "Ouch! I'm finding your mum and telling her that you've been naughty!"

Heidi Gadsden (7)
Christchurch Junior School, Christchurch

Adventures Of The Cute Dog

On a cold night, a dog called Pumpkin was lost in a dark forest. He was very scared. A few hours later, he met a squirrel called Orange. Orange was very kind and thoughtful. Orange found a path that led to a village. They decided to go down it. As they started to go down, they found a beautiful-looking house. Inside the house lived some very nice people who looked like Pumpkin's owners. The people noticed Pumpkin and then noticed Orange. Orange was shocked to see their faces but the people decided to be nice to him.

Lexus Thorn (9)

Christchurch Junior School, Christchurch

Finding An Exciting Place

Once upon a time, there was a girl who wanted to go on an adventure. She saw an amazing place that had lollipops. It was Sweetie Land! She looked around, the grass was sweet and the clouds were cotton candy! She saw someone in the distance, it was a bunny... the Easter Bunny! It was placing eggs, not plastic eggs, chocolate eggs! The girl went to check her wallet, but the coins were chocolate coins! She fell asleep.
When she woke up, she was back home. She looked around, but the bunny had gone...

Ava Fletcher (7)
Christchurch Junior School, Christchurch

The Myth Of The Woods

Once upon a time in Australia, there was a small down called Amagen Town. In Amagen Town, there was a girl called Sophie. Sophie lived with her mum and grandad. One day at school, her friends were talking about a rainforest that was a myth. Sophie was curious about the rainforest, so she told her mum she wanted to go there. When she got there, she found a peacock with a sparkly, golden horn. She wanted to bring it home to her mum and grandad, so she did! Ever since, she was grateful for everything.

Kiko Alexander (7)
Christchurch Junior School, Christchurch

Zerork's Bank Steal

Once there was a monster named Zerork who had a fiery head and a robo-suit. His base was on the moon. Zerork wanted lots of money, so he found a bank on Earth to steal the money from. When he arrived on Earth he shot everything in his way. Everybody was scared. Sean was doing his school play and heard cries for help. He changed into his superhero outfit and went to the bank to stop Zerork. He shot his special wave at Zerork to put out his fiery head. A terrified Zerork flew back to his moon base...

Sean Borrett (7)
Christchurch Junior School, Christchurch

Into The Future

I found a portal in my wardrobe, keeping me awake. I stepped into it and, you'd wish you were there. There was purple and blue dust swirling in the air. The cause of the dust was a bright red Mercedes flying around in the sky as it was breaking into pieces. Suddenly, it stopped in midair. Everyone gathered as a beautiful, red-haired girl stepped out. She was looking for me. She said her name was Ava but that was my name! She was my future self! Wow, strange things could happen with portals...

Ava Rose Righelato (8)
Christchurch Junior School, Christchurch

Exploring A Candy Shop

Once upon a time, there was an explorer called Sweety. One time, she landed in a candy shop. She explored all the shops. When she saw her favourite sweet, she ate it without paying. No one was there so she ate all the sweets. After that, she was so full, she napped but, when she woke up. She saw people and the shop was getting sold! They needed to get all the sweets out. The president let the explorer keep all the sweets. When the explorer went on more adventures, she would get lots of sweets.

Amie Simmonds (8)
Christchurch Junior School, Christchurch

My Unicorn

Once there was a unicorn called Magic. She was very lonely, she lived in an enchanted garden. She was pink, purple and turquoise. She had a sparkly, shiny, silver horn.
Suddenly, I fell down a hole and stepped on a small key. It took me to an enchanted garden. Next, I saw a unicorn whose name was Magic. I said that my name was Alana. We saw some hearts and stars in the sky on our way to the water fountain. I tripped again and found myself back at the hole I'd fallen in before.

Alana Martin (7)
Christchurch Junior School, Christchurch

Super Glitter

One day, Super Glitter had come back from a mission and, as a treat, she went to the yellow beach and got herself a deckchair to lie on. She was about to fall asleep when she heard someone calling for help. She asked what was wrong, but she didn't stop. Then, she saw what was wrong. Her daughter was out at sea! The superhero used her power and Super Glitter's daughter was back to shore. Next, Super Glitter gave her some tea and asked how she got so far. "A wave pushed me into the sea!"

Tylah Scatt (8)
Christchurch Junior School, Christchurch

Exploring Sweety Land

Once upon a time, I travelled to Sweety Land in a time machine. When I got there, I played in the chocolate river. After that, I went inside the gingerbread house. Inside, there was a really jumpy pet pug. I played in the chocolate hot tub next. It was so much fun! After that, I lay in the relaxing hammock. It snapped, so I fell down, down, down! I found that I was back home. When I got home, I did some drawing and went to bed with my teddy, Sunshine. In the morning, I had breakfast.

Emma Rose Dixon (7)
Christchurch Junior School, Christchurch

The Planet Zone

One day, I went to the forest and found a portal. I walked through and, when I came out, I found myself in space. We saw Planet Pluto and it was quite extraordinary. We also saw Jupiter, Saturn, Uranus and Neptune. Then, we saw the rest of the planets. We found a rocket and guess what? We went inside it. We flew back down to Earth, then we all went back home for dinner. We had Planet Pasta and then we went to bed in my bunk bed. I couldn't wait for another adventure!

Elle Halford (8)
Christchurch Junior School, Christchurch

Superheroes Save The Day

Once upon a time, there was a superhero called Ruby. She was the sort of person that would wear jeans. I wouldn't. She lived with her mum, dad and she also had an annoying brother. She lived in a cottage, it was called Mable Cottage. Suddenly, she saw a man stuck on a roof, so she flew in the air and she caught hold of one of the many leaves. She pulled and pulled and pulled. When she finally got the man down, she couldn't believe it. She then went home to bed.

Daisy Tebbutt (8)
Christchurch Junior School, Christchurch

The Mystery Cave

I stepped through the portal, not knowing what to expect, but I saw a small cave entrance. I went into the cave and found a colourful chamber full of children playing. In one corner, there was a hole. I jumped down it and found a spotlight. I started to dance under it, but all of a sudden, a small kitten flew towards me. She was very friendly. I named her Biscuit. She showed me a portal. We went through it and found ourselves back home. Biscuit came to live with me.

Abi Fewings (9)
Christchurch Junior School, Christchurch

Santa's Daughters In The Human Universe

"What's that?" I wondered. There was a round cylinder sticking out of the wall. 'Twist me' it said on the wall. I thought for a minute, should I get Pearl, Dad or Mum? "Pearl!" I shouted.
"What, Crystal?" she replied.
"Come quick, I've found something!"
I twisted it.
"No!" Pearl said.
"A portal?"
"Come on," Pearl said.
We went in and the portal closed. I started to panic. We were stuck! "What are we going to do?"
"Don't ask me, why ask me?" Pearl shouted...

Felicity Concarr (10)
Grantham Preparatory International School, Grantham

Mr Fuzzy

Once upon a time, there was a fluffy ball called Mr Fuzzy. He lived in a tree in the middle of nowhere. He went exploring and went about 100 miles away from the forest and found a village called Whovaville. There was a very tall mountain right next to the village. He saw a big blue door on the snowy mountain and asked, "Who lies up on the peak of the mountain?"
They whispered, "The Grinch..."
Then, Mr Fuzzy stared up the mountain and found out it had 'The Grinch' on the door. Then, he was kicked off the mountain!

Harry Trundley (9)
Grantham Preparatory International School, Grantham

The Great Story Of Monopoly

"Okay," said Sam. "I want Covent Garden." He passed 400 Monopoly money to the banker but, as soon as the money touched the banker's hand, a sudden jerk pulled him forward!

He woke up from his unconsciousness, he was in some sort of city. Sam leant on a tree to recover from his unconsciousness, but it made an odd noise. He decided to give it a little knock. It was hollow! He took out a tissue to wipe his nose but something felt crusty. He had a moustache! There was only one explanation: he was in Monopoly!

Stanley Berry (9)

Grantham Preparatory International School, Grantham

Back In Time

It was a normal day at school. We were doing maths when a siren went off but it wasn't a fire alarm. It was an air raid siren from World War Two! Everyone rushed out and planes went over. We went into an underground tunnel. I was terrified and I passed out.

I woke up on a train with a gas mask and a suitcase, then a woman said to me, "You're finally awake."

"Where am I?" I said in a terrified voice.

"In the country," she said kindly. Then, we arrived in a small village called Poderhill...

Sophia Diamond (9)

Grantham Preparatory International School, Grantham

The Origin Story Of Titan

One day, a man called Kevin visited a nuclear powerplant and looked at the nuclear water. Suddenly, the ground shook and he fell in! The alarm went off. Everyone ran outside.

Two days later, he came out of the water and he ran home. He found out he had superpowers! He decided to work on a really cool suit that could fly. A day later, he tested the suit, it worked! He was the hero of his town, Creeksville, and the news named him Titan. He went on to be a great superhero.

Toby Stuart Micklewright (9)
Grantham Preparatory International School, Grantham

The Shorter Way Home

Guy walked into a dark forest thinking it was a shorter way home. He was really wrong, but he didn't know that. All of a sudden, he fell into a hole! The first thing that came to his mind was that he didn't have any food or water! He started to scream, "Help!" but nobody heard him. He just sat there sulking his eyes out. Then, he started to climb out of the hole. He suddenly heard wolves in the distance. Now he was really scared and nobody had seen him since.

Isobel Allsop (9)
Grantham Preparatory International School, Grantham

Bones!

When I woke up, I had no clue where I was. I looked around, but I saw nobody. I figured I was in a forest. I looked down on myself, I was flabbergasted! I was a skeleton. I sat down to figure everything out. I was a skeleton in a forest with no clue where I was. On a scale of one to ten, this would be a minus three. I ran out of the forest and I saw skeletons with clothes on! One of them said hi. I figured there was only one possible answer. I was dead...

Yuvan Barani (9)
Grantham Preparatory International School, Grantham

Fall Into The Egyptian World

One night, I went to bed and fell through my bed. I was scared and then, I popped out of the other end and landed on my back. I was in Egypt, so I decided to go inside a pyramid and I saw Tutankhamun. He then popped out of the wall and said, "You're trapped. I panicked. He picked me up and put me in a room with dozens of dead people in the room. With my knowledge, I knew that I could get out by pushing the gate... It wouldn't move...

Maddison Wittering (9)

Grantham Preparatory International School, Grantham

The Burger Man

A man had too many burgers and turned into one! This man, or burger, was going to McDonald's to get revenge on the people who wanted to eat him. He hit them with his spatula and squirted tomato sauce at them. The burger man only drank chocolate milkshakes. He had four hot dogs, but actual food hot dogs. His car was called the burgermobile. The burger man met a tomato man and then they finally became friends. They lived happily ever after.

Harry Kennard (10)

Grantham Preparatory International School, Grantham

Hogwarts Mystery...

I know you won't believe me, but I go to Hogwarts! You might think it's easy and fun but lately, the dementors, they're the guards of Hogwarts, attacked Harry! I almost forgot to mention, I am Hermione Granger. The dementors seem to be coming closer to the ground, in through my window, this can't be real but it seems to be! They're now attacking me and I can't fight them off with a spell! It's over...!
It must have just been a dream...

Phoebe Jessop (9)
Grantham Preparatory International School, Grantham

WWI

I woke up. I was in a trench! There were people dead about a metre away from me. Shots fired every second, so I got up. I still had no clue what was going on. I then knew what was going on. I was in a war. I had a rifle, so I went to find a General. I found one and asked, "What should I do?"

He said, "Go to the front line."

I went to the front line. I was going to die. I went up over the top...

Milo Schneider (9)

Grantham Preparatory International School, Grantham

Space Mission

I stepped into the house and found a piece of paper. When I opened it, it had an invention for going into space on it! I went to space, it was amazing. There were loads of scientists. I stepped into the ship and it was colossal. There were people inside. We counted from ten down to one. *Blast off!* We were all in space. Everyone enjoyed it so much, that everyone lived in space!

Elena Adele Scalise (8)
Harwell Primary School, Harwell

The Lost Key

Once upon a time, there lived a little boy named Toshyth. He loved his toy Pikachu, but one day, Pikachu disappeared and Toshyth felt really sad. He searched everywhere but there was no sign of him, so he called the detective and she used her magnifying glass to see. The detective asked Toshyth where he last had Pikachu. Toshyth didn't remember. The detective checked the whole house, but it wasn't there. There was one place she didn't check and it was the bedroom. Pikachu wasn't under the bed, blanket or shelf, but it was under a pillow!

Tanvisri Kota (8)

Holy Cross Catholic Primary School, Liverpool

The Recycling Superhero

Wandering along the empty streets of Abby Mad, I came across a young man who started throwing trash in the recycling bin, screaming about how he doesn't care. I walked towards him, trying to convince him about why he should care. I tried to show him what the world would look like if it was full of trash and we couldn't recycle any of it. He then felt some sympathy towards my words and he wanted to change his ways. He started off by removing the trash he'd placed in the recycling bin and he thanked me for helping him.

Ghalya Esmail (9)
Holy Cross Catholic Primary School, Liverpool

My Vision Of The Future

In the future, there were libraries located under the sea. Let me tell you about Mel's life in 3019. As soon as Mel entered a library, there was a book that attracted her eyes. She couldn't stop herself from reading the book! In no time, she realised it was a magical cookbook. Next, Mel found herself cooking a recipe called Go-Back Banana Bread. She wanted to see what it was like in 2019. Mel had a quick nibble and evaporated right away. When she came back, she was amazed and ready to cook the next recipe!

Jiya Thakkar (9)
Holy Cross Catholic Primary School, Liverpool

The Unknown Phone

Jeremy was a twelve-year-old kid who bought a phone. One gloomy night, he had a very strange phone call. It said 'unknown caller'.

The next morning, Jeremy found a paper and there were dates on it. He called Sherlock Holmes, the detective. Jeremy showed him the paper. The detective knew who it was. It was a man named Mark License. Sherlock Holmes knew where he was.

Sherlock and Watson found Mark and gave him to the police, then Jeremy was safe and sound forever.

Rishiraj Das (8)
Holy Cross Catholic Primary School, Liverpool

The Last Mermaid City

Felicity slowly walked across the thin ice to her home in the North Pole. Suddenly, she heard the ice begin to crack and she fell through. The water was ice cold and started to drag her away from the home she'd made.

She saw something swimming towards her. Could it be a shark? No, it was a mermaid! The mermaid had a beautiful light pink tail and gave Felicity the power to breathe underwater! The mermaid showed Felicity the lost city of Atlantis and took her home.

India Cowell (9)

Holy Cross Catholic Primary School, Liverpool

The Wonders Of Emerald Forest

In Emerald Forest lived a joyful unicorn called Daisy. One day, Daisy awoke to see that with every blink, the flowers disappeared into the crisp grass. Every time this happened, golden glitter puffed from the ground. Daisy leapt with excitement.

As she was searching for where the flowers had vanished to, she was shocked to find a family of fairies sitting on the magical, rainbow-coloured toadstools. "Wow!" she exclaimed.

At the end of the most exciting day, after making new best friends, Daisy realised how wonderful her home really was. She wanted to explore it all!

Bebe Scarlett Lansdown (10)

Hundon Community Primary School, Hundon

Mischief Boy

"Here we go again..."

"Danny!"

I ran faster than my legs could go until I regretfully looked back. Raging towards me was Mrs White. I leapt into the portal to escape that horrible nightmare. I stumbled through the other end of the portal, came out on North Street, where I live!

I wandered down to my house and peered through the kitchen window. My perfect little sister was being told off by Mum. I turned and went back to the street, where a policeman was stealing a bike from a little girl.

What has happened! Why's everyone being so bad?

Amy Harper (10)

Hundon Community Primary School, Hundon

The Princess Superhero

In a town of horrible people, a princess named Daisy longed to be a superhero. One day, a thief stole money from the bank and escaped the police in the nick of time as Daisy watched him run away. She decided to jump into action and catch the thief herself. She went through dark alleys and creepy buildings, wet lanes and abandoned houses until she finally caught him. "Hey, you!" she bellowed. "Drop the money and come with me, you're in trouble!"

A little while later, he went to prison and Daisy handed the money back. She was a superhero!

Niamh Mitson (9)

Hundon Community Primary School, Hundon

Spook Land

That long-awaited, cold, dingy night of the second of February has come around again. Two rings of the church bells chime with the loud but distant cries that follow. As Joe entered the wrecked, spooky house, he heard something creaky behind him. He kept hearing strange noises that sounded like ghosts floating by his ear. As quick as a flash, he saw a miniature door that led into the devil's woods. As Joe squeezed himself through the miniature door, he spotted a colossal woods that was pitch-black inside. As he looked around, he saw something in the distance...

Finley Simpson (10)
Hundon Community Primary School, Hundon

The Good Monster

I was conducting some experiment in the science lab. The chemicals mixed together and exploded into a massive portal. I stepped nervously through. It led me to a deserted world. I noticed my body transforming into a werewolf. What was happening? Just then, an army of spooky monsters jumped out of nowhere! A thunderous noise came running through my ears, so I looked up and there were aliens coming out of a cubed object in the sky, trying to access the portal. The monsters and I fought for hours and we won the battle to save mankind and future civilisations...

George Speller (9)
Hundon Community Primary School, Hundon

The Next Life

An eleven-year-old girl named Camiliar stood in shock. A bright portal was in front of her. One month ago, she was worrying about her SATs, but now she had a million questions that needed to be answered about this portal. Without looking back, she stepped in. Screens, bright screens surrounded her. Each one turning on. She looked confused and scared as if she was about to have a heart attack. She could see her future in her head, Camiliar's SATs, schools and everything in the blink of an eye. "Hello," said a creepy voice from a bright screen...

Lola-Rose Slater (10)
Hundon Community Primary School, Hundon

The Fallout Room

The day was hot, Dave stood outside a bar. He was trying to get revenge on Richard, the man who annoyed him. He got a bit of gold. When the guard said, "Sorry kid, you're only eleven years old," it really angered Dave, so he hurled the guard across the bar. He then picked up a pool cue and whacked the lock off the back door. Inside, there were his teachers!

"You ruined our game!" the headteacher exclaimed.

"Save it, Richard!" Dave shouted. He went up to him with his fists. Cards went everywhere, then Dave woke up.

Thomas Jeggo (11)
Hundon Community Primary School, Hundon

The Finish Line

I felt the sun blazing on my back as I zoomed past all my friends and family. They cheered for me. "Go on Grace, you're in the lead!" As my family cheered for me with pride, the feeling was like a flower that had opened and felt amazing. When I finally crossed the finish line, I couldn't stop running. My legs hurt, my arms hurt, everywhere hurt. I didn't stop running because I didn't want to let my family or friends down. When I finally stopped running, my heart was racing... First place! I couldn't believe it.

Grace Daniels (10)
Hundon Community Primary School, Hundon

Dragon Rescue

The dragon land was so high in the sky, it was almost invisible. It had candyfloss trees and sticky syrup rivers. One day, there was a thunderous rumble and their world began to descend from the sky with a huge crash because the volcano erupted and acted like a jetpack! Escaping dragons bolted in all directions. Sadly, a young dragon got stuck under a massive rock. Every dragon was trying to save it. The magma and lava dragons diverted the magma and lava. Finally, they just managed to get the young dragon out before their fire ran out...

Marisol Brown (9)

Hundon Community Primary School, Hundon

The Red Rescue

It was my first mission to Mars. As Captain, I was responsible for landing the ship with my co-pilot Samany. The landing went smoothly and we decided to explore, but when we climbed out of the ship, we saw a vague figure in the distance. As we neared the figure, we were stunned that it was the missing astronaut who had disappeared in 2008. This expedition had now turned into a rescue mission! We led him back to the ship and prepared for lift-off. As I turned around, the missing astronaut's eyes were glowing red. Who had we rescued?

Riley George Morgan-Jones (9)
Hundon Community Primary School, Hundon

The Future

On a regular Sunday, a boy called Jacomb could see into the future. He didn't tell anybody about it. He had to do a science project on Wednesday, that was when he was going to tell everyone. When he went into the future, he discovered... robots were going to take over the world! He told everyone about it and they all prepared.

It was the day of the robot detonation. People grabbed their gear and fought. When Jacomb came across the boss robot, he pulled out a stick and killed him. But then, Jacomb realised it wasn't the boss...

Harvey Richardson-Capoling (10)
Hundon Community Primary School, Hundon

The Ghost Spooks

As I sat in my small bedroom, playing with my toy dog, I saw my small monkey blink. "My toy's alive!" I yelled at the top of my voice.

"What do you mean 'my toy's alive'?" bellowed his mum as she shot up the stairs.

"Look, Mum!" I cried. We looked closely at the miniature monkey on the corner of my bed. Then, it blinked again. We both screamed at the top of our lungs. All of a sudden, it talked! What was it saying? I panicked. Was this Mum playing a trick on me or was it real?

Erin May Jeggo (9)
Hundon Community Primary School, Hundon

The Blinding Black Hole

I spun over and over, swirling into the black vortex. Then, suddenly, a white glow flashed and my eyes went up. The white figure blinded my eyes and I was gone.

Later on, I woke up only to find myself surrounded by chunks of debris and active radioactive vortexes, trying to suck up items as well as me. Then, a hole appeared behind me and I ran. As I made it there, it grabbed me and pulled me... Filled with joy, I checked my bearings and realised I was in another galactical universe. I thought to myself... *No!*

Grae Mileham (11)
Hundon Community Primary School, Hundon

Jump Man And The Planet Killer

Jump Man has a foe called Planet Killer who wanted to destroy Earth. Jump Man had a super jump and strength.

One day, in the city, everyone felt a push. Jump Man knew it was his foe, so he jumped high up and grabbed Planet Killer. They fought for ages. Finally, they both fell back to Earth but, before Jump Man could realise, he was on the ground. Planet Killer was gone, he'd disappeared in the city! Jump Man was so mad, he searched long and hard for Planet Killer. Two days later, Jump Man gave up.

Harper George Porter Tabrar (9)

Hundon Community Primary School, Hundon

The Other Side

"We need to get in the bus!"

"The bus? That's what's causing these things!" shouted Ryan over the noise of the machine in the bus in a field.

"If we can get to the bus, we can shut off the machine, but we have to be careful," Chris whispered to Ryan.

The two men thought and thought and thought until Ryan had an idea. "We should dress up as one so we can sneak past."

"Good idea Ryan." The two men found something to make their costumes. They sneaked past and pressed the button...

Alex Sharpe (10)
Hundon Community Primary School, Hundon

A Devil In The Future

A girl who was a devil was running. She was running from a psycho! This girl's name was Eleanor, who was me! Unfortunately, I ran in the forest, losing all my confidence, not like I had some before... Something would cheer me up. I saw a door, it was red but I went inside. I was suddenly in the future. I looked around for help or if anyone was there. After hours of looking, I found my best friend and suddenly, stopping me from passing was a creature screaming. Was I ever going to leave?

Amelie Sullivan (10)
Hundon Community Primary School, Hundon

Taking The Destroyer

As the ship moved closer we deployed a tractor beam. The door of the destroyer opened. I put on my rocket pack and flew in, but the crew of the destroyer knew I was coming. However, I had my laser zapper, but I had to navigate through a very long tunnel. It led me to the docking bay and their ships. "Hey, stop right there!" someone shouted. "No!" I laughed. "I've got what I came for!" I zoomed back out through the tunnel.

Gabriel Parker-Hall (9)
Hundon Community Primary School, Hundon

One Crazy Yet Foody Christmas

As I jumped in the portal, I could see a candy cane bridge hovering over a frosting river. Heading over the bridge, there was a gingerbread castle with gumdrops as doors. Before I could finish, a colossal one was stood in front of me. I rolled up my sleeves and began to eat.

An eternity later, I had finished the fight. All of a sudden, I arrived home. I ran up to my mum and dad and gave them a hug. I was happy to be home for Christmas.

Perdita Maisie Jones (11)
Hundon Community Primary School, Hundon

Unknown

The fluorescent strings of yellow knitted the sky, almost dusk, the crime that took place in the soul-grasping woods disturbed by a brave soul. The clues indicate claws; sharp claws. Queuing suspects, guilt captured inside them, unreleasable. Blood dripping in the crime scene. Witnesses refused to give empirical evidence. Dusk breaks down like cracked, shattered glass. Scimitar blades sharpened. Fear released out of the investigating officers, hearing the sound. Simultaneously, the suspects began to pull their hair paranoidly. Within seconds, dawn opened. Two wandering citizens entered the death zone, picking up the helmet. 'Head of officers (county jail)' it read.

Nakshatra Manasani (10)
London Meed CP School, Burgess Hill

Secret Silhouette

Overhead, the night sky rumbled like a hungry child's stomach. Lightning flashed, illuminating the house that stood deathly still in the distance. Bats soared from side to side, then clung to the bare trees. House lights were off but it was well-known someone was in there. One brave adventurer approached with caution, yet determined to resolve the conspiracy theory, all in black, matching the sky. He crept forward. A shiver of fear ran down his spine. One step at a time, he reached his destination. Glancing up, he saw a silhouette. He blinked and blinked again...

Imogen Porter (11)
London Meed CP School, Burgess Hill

Haven't You Heard?

The rusty machine rattled and clanked, flinging me everywhere in the little space I had. The iron door creaked open and I entered a world of dismal houses and dark, never-ending streets.
Everything was isolated, save one boy huddled in an alley, sobbing. Coming closer, I called to him. He looked up. "Haven't you heard?" he bawled. "The world is ending!"
With a flash of lightning, he vanished. I had to go back, otherwise, the world would explode with me in it.
One small problem, the time machine had vanished into thin air...

Verity Collins (11)
London Meed CP School, Burgess Hill

The Fearless Boy

He grabbed the sword, having gained impeccable strength. He was now ready to slay the dragon who had killed his father five years ago. He travelled far and wide to reach this deep, dark dungeon. One step inside, his eyes adjusted to the gloom. Fearful of what happened to his father, he took another step forward. All of a sudden, a ferocious flame shot past his face. Emerging out of the darkness, a huge beast lurched forward. This young boy faced his ultimate fear, then dipped his sword into the nearby lava and thrust it upwards, slaying the dragon dead.

Archie Townsend (11)

London Meed CP School, Burgess Hill

The Missing Boy

This could have been his last day ever. The momentum of him being launched off his bike sent him tumbling down the hill. He came to a halt. It was a pile of dirt.

In the morning, the town sherriff decided to search for the missing boy. He found the boy's bike and immediately knew where he was. He bolted down the hill and found his baseball cap. He looked around and saw a child's hand sticking out of a pile of dirt. He ran over to it. He pulled and pulled. He pulled a bit more... *Bang!*

Leo Rimmer (11)
London Meed CP School, Burgess Hill

Key Mystery

One misty day, the Baker family went on a walk around the fields near their house as they did every other Sunday. They were close friends with the field owner. He had asked them to dig up a hole to make a lake. As they were digging, they found a key. They went to ask their family about it. First, they went to Aunty Carly and Uncle Tim, but they had no idea. Next, the Bakers went to Nan and Grandad. Did they know anything? Nan didn't, but Grandad... he knew something. He wouldn't tell them!

Grace Lily Chambers (10)
London Meed CP School, Burgess Hill

The Secret

Burying Mr Mystery was extremely difficult. The soil was hard and it all stuck together so the spade was useless. I had to use my hands and it was the worst feeling ever because it went up my fingernails! Mr Mystery was the only person who knew the secret to life on Earth. Since he died, people tried to find it out, but his protective ghost would attack. One night, all the trees around his grave died and disintegrated into dust. The ghost of Mr Mystery slowly rose from the ground and whispered...

Sophie Stacey (11)
London Meed CP School, Burgess Hill

The Project

The day of the school project was nearly over. We had to make a robot to help someone else. Ours gave answers to everything. After school, we decided to test our robot out. We switched it on and... it worked! Its eyes lit up and it talked. It would only talk and move when you told it to, or so we thought. Someone needed to take it home. I was the one. I folded it up and put it into my bag, but I forgot to zip it up. Little did I know that it was alive... It moved!

Phoebe Brown (10)
London Meed CP School, Burgess Hill

The Black Hole

Flying to the moon in my enormous, blue spaceship, I came across three aliens. I was amazed at what I saw. Rubbing my eyes, I looked again at the aliens. They had three eyes each and little blobs floating above their heads. I flew closer to hear them and nervously listened. *Blob! Blob! Blob!* came from the mouths of the aliens. They flew further away because they were a bit scared of my blue colossal spaceship. I shouted to them, "There's nothing to be afraid of!" and invited them to my spaceship. We became friends and returned to Earth together.

Taha Karegar (8)
Millway Primary School, Duston

The Ghost Girl

Kitty came down from her bedroom to talk to her mum and dad but, for some reason, they weren't there. Kitty looked around the whole house, but they weren't there. Suddenly, the power went off. She started to get a shiver down her spine. A voice started to talk to her. It said, "If you want your parents back, you have to find them."
She was wondering if she should get out of the house, but the doors were locked. "Help!" she screamed, but no one came. The ghost finally showed herself and disappeared again...

Eloise Baker (8)
Millway Primary School, Duston

The Mystery Thief

Captain Heropants stood proud. High in the sky, he watched the town. Then, suddenly, a car alarm went off so Captain Heropants dove from the sky, but the thief had a massive head start! Captain Heropants' trusty sidekick, Piggy Hero the hamster, flew out of nowhere and gave Captain Heropants his super bionic boots and got mini super bionic boots for himself. They both then chased after the thief, Bob. Bob ran for his life but he was tripped over by Piggy Hero. and got grabbed by Captain Heropants. There was someone else nearby...

Jasmyn-Rae McDonald (8)
Millway Primary School, Duston

The Evil Bear

I was in my bedroom relaxing until I heard a noise. I ignored it and carried on drawing. I felt nervous. I finished drawing my picture, so I put it behind me. I remembered that I didn't draw the sun on my picture. I turned around to get my picture and realised that my picture wasn't there. I was confused. I went downstairs to tell my parents. When I came back upstairs, my teddy was running around the room with my picture. I felt terrified. The teddy ran after me. It was terrifying, my teddy was alive!

Edmund Puchovic (8)
Millway Primary School, Duston

Superhero Saves The World

Once there was a brave, strong superhero that had brilliant superpowers. Suddenly, in China, there was a huge fire which could kill a lot of people, so the brilliant, clever hero flew to save the innocent, sad people from the steamy, smoky fire. He used his firepower to save them. "Oh no!" he said sadly. He flew to Beijing. He saw a splendid house that was on fire. As he was passing the house, he saw a small six-year-old girl. He flew to her and saved her from the fire and then, he flew back home.

Oliwier Gronski (8)
Millway Primary School, Duston

Don't Move!

I froze. Something was lurking in the attic. I stood up from the priceless antique chair and strolled to the bottom of the creaky stairs. *It's probably my mind playing tricks on me*, I thought. As soon as I turned around, the walking got louder. I thought it was a joke, so I went upstairs, not knowing it was actually real. I just went upstairs, it was like a horror movie. I didn't care. I climbed up the glossy pull-down stairs to the attic and was shocked when I saw a man...

Peaches-Blossom June Gooding (9)
Millway Primary School, Duston

The Dino

One night, I got sucked up into a hole. I opened my eyes and I was in a dino nest. The first thing I saw were eggs, then I heard stomps. I ran as fast as I could up the volcano. I looked back at the nest and I saw a spinosaurus, it was huge! Then, a T-rex came charging at me and actually saved me. I was surprised! I was in luck, but a herd of spinosaurus came. I got dropped off in the centre of the island. I wanted to go home right now!

Lucas Smith (8)
Millway Primary School, Duston

Vanish

Hi, I'm Nikki. Me and my friends : Lily, Ski, Izzy, Amy and Kat have just finished the most boring lesson ever: two-hour maths! Well, I suppose science is also rather boring...

We went to our secret hideout. When we got there, a terrible thing happened. Mrs Eagle-eye, the headteacher had been waiting for us. "Oh no!" I said. Izzy almost fainted.

"Well then girls," Mrs Eagle-eye said, "time to disappear!" Then, Ski, Izzy, Lily, Kat and Amy disappeared. "Now you!" she said and she waved her cane and then she said, "Disappear, disappear!" and I vanished...

Aminah Khan (9)
Normanton House School, Derby

My Unicorn Amber

My magic unicorn, Amber, is beautiful and has a long, wavy and colourful mane. She can fly in the air. She wears golden shoes with jewels in the middle. She's everyone's favourite unicorn. Only one person hated her, he hates all unicorns. Wizard Meanio.

One day, he trapped poor Amber in a cage! She couldn't get out until a thought struck her mind. She got the magic spell book and chanted a get out spell. "Help me, get out, oh please set me free. Let me see!"

Suddenly, she was free! When she came home, she got 100 treats!

Eshaal Shahzad (9)

Normanton House School, Derby

Adventure

I went on a boat, it was white. The sail was rainbow-coloured. Then, a mysterious hole came. It was big, black and had white spots. I went inside, realising what it was. I thought, *am I back in time?* A surprising adventure was waiting for me. I was really shocked. The dinosaur world was colourful with different dinosaurs: Tyrannosaurus, diplodocus, triceratops... I made a friend: a diplodocus. I didn't know when I'd go home. Suddenly, I went into the hole. I was back. It was night-time, so I went to sleep...

Naafi Bin Naeem (9)

Normanton House School, Derby

All About Pilchald

Long, long ago, there was a brave cat called Pilchald. He was a big cat and he was fierce and amazing and my hero. He saw bad guys and I helped him to defeat the bad guys. I gave him a warm bed, bath, clothes, hat and belt to say thank you. We played together and read a book together. I jumped with him too. Pilchald looked out the window and saw bad guys stealing from a jewellery shop. He ran out and jumped on them. They dropped the bag and ran. Pilchald was a hero!

Zahra Sohail (7)
Normanton House School, Derby

The Solar System Football Cup

In this amazing tournament, all eight planets would compete with each other for a chance to be the first Solar System Champions. Earth would be represented by our best footballers like Ronaldo, Messi, Neymar, Neuer and Ibrahimović.

Earth's first match was against the aliens of Saturn who used their best players from Titan. The match was exciting, but Saturn were no match for Earth's finest.

Earth's next opponents were the Martians of Mars. This was the final match to crown the first champions. Ronaldo scored with a bicycle kick in the dying seconds to win and crown Earth the champions.

Usmaan Parvez (9)

Roe Green Junior School, Kingsbury

The Boastful Impala

Once upon a dry Savannah there lived an impala. She bragged too much. She was always admiring herself. All the other animals hated her.

One day, when she was passing the watering hole, a crocodile snapped its jaws at her. "Why are you so boastful? I'm tired of it!" shouted the crocodile. "Ah, you're so mean! Get out of my way!" she screamed. The crocodile went back into the water. The impala ran as fast as she could. Suddenly, she bumped into a gigantic boulder. Unexpectedly, the boulder rolled and squashed her. That was the end of that impala.

Rupin Bakrania (8)
Roe Green Junior School, Kingsbury

The Creeper

It was a scary night. Me and Preesha were alone, suddenly, the door creaked open and a creeper came running towards us. So, we ran away but then I found I was wearing diamond armour and it was enchanted, along with my pickaxe, sword, bow and arrow. We ran to my friend's house. You know why? Because it was made of obsidian and I asked him, "Louie, can I talk to you?"
"Yes, sure!"
I told Louie everything.
Then Louie said, "Run towards it and when it's about to explode, run away!"
I did as told and defeated the creeper.

Preet Pravin Hirani (9)
Roe Green Junior School, Kingsbury

Melody's Adventure

Melody stepped into the dark, gloomy woods. She looked through something shiny and, suddenly, it became brighter, brighter and brighter. Animals crawled and swung from tree to tree. Then, Melody saw a bridge and she started walking on the bridge. But, the bridge was about to collapse, so she quickly jumped onto the other end. She got covered in leaves and smelt like leaves. So, she kept on walking and walking but there was no one there. After a while, she saw a lion coming towards her and she quickly ran. She jumped over the bridge and she was safe!

Chahat Piyushbhai Patel (9)
Roe Green Junior School, Kingsbury

The Girl Who Liked To Bake Muffins

One bright sunny morning on Twinkle Lane, a twelve-year-old girl named Shiny was baking some delicious cherry muffins for the school fair. The smell was out of this world!

The muffins looked amazing and they were very popular and sold out very fast. Shiny's friend Jessie was the biggest fan of her muffins and bought three. Shiny was happy her muffins sold well but was also sad she had nothing left to sell.

Jessie had an idea and said, "Why don't you bake some more and sell them at my mum's market stall? I would buy one every day!"

Neya Patel (7)

Roe Green Junior School, Kingsbury

Nowhere

I was going round in circles as I tried to figure out where I was. With no visualisation of my vicinity, my situation was impenetrable. I had almost given up my aspiration to find a way out when I realised I was descending through the air with the smell of repugnance entering my nose and wind constantly rushing towards me. It was hard to suppress my shrill shrieks as a meteor nearly collided with my frenzied fingers. My blinking eyelids disobeyed me. As I plummeted towards my fatal fall, I would never forget the vague outline of what I saw...

Safiyah Uddin (9)
Roe Green Junior School, Kingsbury

New World

Before Christmas, I decided to help my mother bring down the decorations from the attic. When I was looking, I found a mysterious box with a silver lock. The key was stuck under the box! Inside was a magic book. I started to read two or three lines, then I realised I was very far from my world. I couldn't see or hear anything from the world I left. It was a mysterious world with strange animals and witches. They didn't hurt me because they couldn't fight with real people, just listen to them. It was a very exciting adventure!

Alexandra Bosnea (7)

Roe Green Junior School, Kingsbury

Adventure Of Space

One day, I went to go to space so I took my rocket ship but before I got to space, I had to fill up the gas and get inside of the rocket. I got ready to blast off in, "Three... two... one... zero, blast off!" Then the gas finished so we landed on the moon. Then a spaceship zoomed around space. It landed on the moon, it was an alien! I went to the alien and said, "Hello, alien!"
The alien said, "Hello!"
I said, "My gas ran out, can I use yours?"
"Yes!" said the alien.

Saiswin Thusyanthan (7)
Roe Green Junior School, Kingsbury

The Very Powerful Superhero

Once upon a time, there was a very powerful superhero called Captain Sparkle. She was very clever because she made her own weapons and jewellery out of gold, silver, bronze and, most importantly, glitter.

One day, she went to the special robot museum which had a big factory. She grew her secret antidote that fought all the evil in the city. On that day, she got a call from a scientist. He said that there were dinosaurs attacking the city! She rushed over to the middle of the city and told the dinosaurs to go back in their cages!

Stefania Antonesi (8)

Roe Green Junior School, Kingsbury

The Haunted House

One night, a man called Sinom was looking for a hotel and he saw a haunted house. He stopped the driver and walked in the house and the door closed by itself. Sinom quickly walked up the stairs and saw a picture moving its eyes! Sinom's heart stopped and he ran upstairs and shut the door. Then he heard a ghost's call. It said, "Sinom! Sinom! Where are you? Sinom!" The ghost came out of the wooden boards on the floor and locked the door and the ghost crept closer and closer. Finally, she killed Sinom and she went.

Darius Bobieca (9)
Roe Green Junior School, Kingsbury

My Trip To Space

One day, I wanted to go on a space trip, so I made a rocket ship and packed up my stuff. To make the rocket ship, I used metal, rocks, wood and glass for the windows. Once I finished, I blasted off to space. "One, two, three, blast off!" I said to myself. Whoopee! Jumping up and down, I approached space. I saw one thousand aliens. I was frightened and shocked. They were glowing and galloping and their frightening faces were toxic, so I went back home. I went inside the rocket ship. "One, two, three, blast off!"

Sara Maria Ungureanu (8)

Roe Green Junior School, Kingsbury

Dinosaur Adventure

I was on a plane, going on an adventure. The adventure was a dinosaur adventure. We saw dinosaurs going around and through the whole place. When we went outside, a T-rex saw us. Then we were so scared and frightened and went inside. Then we were so sleepy and went to bed.

The next morning, we ate breakfast then went in the car and drove. When we were driving, a dinosaur ate our car, but we survived. Next, when our car was eaten, we had to walk the whole time backwards and forward. Finally, we reached our cousin's house.

Samuel Horandau (7)
Roe Green Junior School, Kingsbury

Coconut Tree

On his trip to Dubai, Akshay saw beautiful coconut trees. He got a strong desire to grow such a tree near his home in India. He made an effort but failed to grow it. Disappointed, he cried. An angel appeared in his dreams and said, "I will not let this tree grow here because I want to teach you something. Just as this tree grows only in a certain place, every child's born with a unique quality. Parents must try and find out that special quality in them and let them grow and develop that quality at their own pace!"

Riyaan Adams (8)
Roe Green Junior School, Kingsbury

The Strange Encounter

One Christmas night, the breezy air hovering over me, my eyes seemed to lay themselves upon a peculiar place. I stumbled like a fever in a dream towards it. There, I saw a misty shadow of a reindeer. Could it have been? Was it real? But, my eyes were not fooling around. In front of me stood the one and only person I'd dreamed of. My ears led me to the soft, soothing sound of bells. I began to touch it when *beep, beep!* My ears were ringing. My alarm clock! Could this have all been an extraordinary, lovely dream?

Nandika Agarwal (9)
Roe Green Junior School, Kingsbury

Welcome To Superhero High School

When you wake up, you probably don't expect a bird appearing at the speed of light! It flew through my window and dropped a letter, and now I knew why the bird was so fast - it was the familiar of one of the greatest heroes of all time! I knew immediately that I was accepted to Superhero High School! After all my tests and trials, finally, today was my day.

The next morning, I leapt out of bed into my school uniform and, when I ran to school, I saw my teacher.

"Welcome to Superhero High School!"

Ifeoluwa Coker (11)

Roe Green Junior School, Kingsbury

Space Mission

When I was playing with my favourite space toys, something weird happened. I realised I was the size of a toy and I was sitting in my own spaceship! After some time, my rocket landed on some strange planet that looked like cheese. When I looked through the window, I saw an alien sitting next to his spaceship, being sad. I went over to say, "What's wrong?"

The alien said, "My spaceship is broken. Can you help me?"

I agreed to mend his spaceship. The alien gave a special rock to me and we went back home.

Sami Raza (7)
Roe Green Junior School, Kingsbury

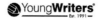

Woodland

In the deep dark woods in a deep dark house with a deep dark cellar lived a scary old witch. However, one day, a girl called Kiya went wandering in the woods, looking for a magical leaf which made people disappear - but she got lost and was found by the scary old witch who said, "I will turn you into my big black cat and keep you forever as a best friend!"

Magically, Kiya found the magic leaf just in time before the witch cast the spell on her! She made the witch disappear and lived happily ever after.

Kiya Gami (7)
Roe Green Junior School, Kingsbury

The Princess, Elf And The Mysterious Egg

Once upon a time, there lived a girl and a boy. The boy was an elf and the girl was a princess. Then the princess found an egg. She called her older sister, Lenzzie. Then she said, "Hey sis, do you know what kind of egg this is?"

"Oh, yes! This is a dragon egg!" Later, they saw a crack on the egg. After, it cracked fully. Then they saw a baby pterodactyl. The pterodactyl saw the princess first so it thought she was its mum. It kept following the princess and the elf took it to its home.

Aruvi Niranjan (9)
Roe Green Junior School, Kingsbury

The Lost Rabbit

Once, there was a girl called Lilly and she had a rabbit, her name was Bloomy. The rabbit went to the circus and they saw a clown. Suddenly, Bloomy got lost. She tried to find the way but she could not get there. She saw the clown. She asked the clown if he had seen her but he hadn't seen her. Bloomy was upset. She started crying. Then, she saw footprints. It was midnight, so she just followed the footprints. Then, she got to her house. She was there! Lilly made a surprise because it was her birthday!

Hadiya Habib (7)
Roe Green Junior School, Kingsbury

The Wonderland

That evening, I thought about Wonderland. It was beautiful and wonderful, except for one thing. The station was broken so that we couldn't use it but, before, it was amazing. One day, I went to the station and saw a broken train inside. It was very old. I felt a bit sleepy, so I had a deep sleep and had a dream. I was in another place, it was cool. It had cars and high-quality buildings and I saw a person who said to come in. I said, "I'll look around the house!" It was actually a dream.

Abdul Rasheed Ahmed (9)
Roe Green Junior School, Kingsbury

Back To Extinction

I was sleeping when I touched my watch and went back in time. It took me back to when dinosaurs lived. It was boiling hot and I was searching for water. I fell unconscious. When I woke up, I saw three dinosaurs standing over me. They were saying words I couldn't even understand. I was probably too tired to know what they were doing to me. It was some kind of spell that automatically healed me. I awoke and I felt like a new person just waiting to explore all around. I hoped I would get home safely!

Laiqah Batool (10)
Roe Green Junior School, Kingsbury

Adventure

This morning, I woke up. My mum said, "Go and explore today."
I went exploring. It was an adventure. I had so much fun. While I was walking, I heard a sound from the long green bushes. It was a squirrel with a long tail wiggling out.
I kept walking. I was so hungry! Luckily, I bought a snack with me. I ate my snack and drank water with it.
I was walking and kept on taking pictures. A lot of the time, I would look around and find my brother. He was with me. It was funny and fun!

Iman Ahmed (8)
Roe Green Junior School, Kingsbury

The World

I stepped into the Nether Portal, hoping I'd find, well, the Nether. I started to feel very woozy. Maybe it was that hot dog I had for lunch? How very wrong I was. I jumped out of the portal, knowing that this was my stop. I was in a cave, similar to the one I'd found this portal in. I led my way up. The grass was green and the trees were blooming. Just up ahead, I could see a village. How delighted I was. I was well on my way to the village. Then, creatures started attacking...

Prem Dave (10)
Roe Green Junior School, Kingsbury

Off Into Space

One morning, I just woke up and I saw I had turned green, my comfy bed was floating and it was hotter than normal. I went downstairs to tell Mom but she was the same as me. I went outside but just before I stepped out, I realised my house was in space. I closed the door just before I ran out of breath. This was a catastrophe! I sadly cried. Green tears came out and I screamed, "I wish I was home!" Then, *whoosh!* I was home! Oh, I was so happy! That was real magic.

Monisha Kerai (9)
Roe Green Junior School, Kingsbury

The Haunted House

One night, on Halloween, I rang a doorbell on a spooky house for some sweets. Suddenly, the door opened but, in my sight, no one was to be seen. There were ghost pictures on the walls and blood all over the floor. Then I crept into a room and in the corner, I saw a scary ghost. It started chasing me. Then I saw an open window and jumped through and fell on the floor. I hurt my knee and I woke up on the floor and found out I'd fallen off my bed and realised it was a nightmare.

Hasan Mohamed Rizath (9)

Roe Green Junior School, Kingsbury

Mysterious Magic

One day, I went to a museum. There was a 'blow your mind' section which sounded interesting, so I went to explore. There was a man sitting in rags and a wand sat next to him, twinkling like a star. Maybe he would blow our minds as he was in the 'blow your mind' section. There were empty chairs, so I sat in, wondering what he would do. When my behind hit the seat, he picked up his wand, stood up and a crowd came. When he pulled the wand from his sleeve, his grin was wicked...

Reiko McDonald (8)
Roe Green Junior School, Kingsbury

Time Travel

One day, when I woke up, I was in a cave. I went outside and saw people in stone trousers. I looked at my clothes and they were stone clothes. I thought very hard about what could have brought me back to the Stone Age. I remembered my mum told me to sleep on a new bed last night. Could that have made me go back to the Stone Age? Then I saw a time machine in front of me. I went inside the machine. I felt dizzy and I couldn't move. Then, all of a sudden, I was home.

Janice Wong (7)
Roe Green Junior School, Kingsbury

The Adventure Underground

I was just sitting on a seat, hanging out with my friend called James. We were in the DLR. We were pretending to be drivers on the seats and we had fun.

Six minutes later, the train ran out of battery and turned off. The doors were open and we went out of the train to explore. My brother said that there was treasure there somewhere and he gave me a map. It was a treasure map! We were over the mark and we dug until we saw treasure. We saw jewels!

David Bordei (7)
Roe Green Junior School, Kingsbury

Sandstorm

I was woken up in a sandstorm in a desert when I was asleep. In the morning, I explored the desert so I could find help. I was in a desert with no food or water, all alone. So, I got scared when I heard rumbling from the edge of a mountain. I was leaping off a pillar in the sandstorm. I could not breathe. So, I stopped and had a nap. Soon, it was night, so I went to a cosy place. While I was waiting at night, I heard something. It was a dream!

Ghulam Mustafa (9)
Roe Green Junior School, Kingsbury

Best Friends

Once upon a time, there lived a unicorn called Sugar and a kangaroo called Jumpy. They lived in Haribo Land. They ate Haribo for dinner as always and asked what they should do. They decided to play adventurers. After they played adventurers, they found a little girl called Icy. They soon became best friends.

One day, they were playing tag. Suddenly, a person called Bubbler appeared. He put a bubble around the trio. In the bubble, they all exclaimed, "Help!" But, Icy stayed calm. She used her ice powers and saved them and then never saw Bubbler again!

Coco Kexin He (7)
St Cuthbert's Primary School, Glasgow

Unicorn Adventure

One day, there was a beautiful purple unicorn. Her name was Ellie May. She went on an adventure to Candyland. When she got to Candyland, she really couldn't believe it. The grand trees were blue bubblegum, the leaves were strawberry jam doughnuts. Ellie did not want to leave because she met other beautiful unicorns. Ellie and her friends went on a walk to find all the beautiful, lovely sweets. Ellie wanted to find a candyfloss ice cream. After a walk in the bubblegum grass, they found a park with all kinds of flavoured candyfloss, including the one she loved!

Elizabeth (6)

St Cuthbert's Primary School, Glasgow

Candy Land

One day, a magical rainbow unicorn called Zara went on an adventure with her best friend. The journey was to explore Candyland. Candyland was a place full of yummy sweeties. Zara wanted to eat a blueberry cupcake. She took the first bite and it tasted yummy. She couldn't stop eating it! The final bite tasted very disgusting. Her face screwed up and she made funny faces. Zara felt very sick and dizzy. Her head was spinning round and round. She fell down and fell asleep and started to dream about an evil witch taking over Candyland.

Yostina Yemane (7)
St Cuthbert's Primary School, Glasgow

The Dangerous Mission Of Two Spy Ninjas

One day, two ninjas arrived in ancient Egypt. They were hungry from the long journey. They found some small apples on the sand. They wondered if they would be poisonous. They did not eat the apples because they knew they would be poisoned. They ran up toward the pyramid door. They tried to push it. A sign appeared. *You must eat.* The ninjas looked at the apples again, and took small bites and closed their eyes. They swallowed the first bit. The golden door creaked open. The ninjas walked slowly into the deep, dark pyramid...

Joshua Wilson Albert (7)
St Cuthbert's Primary School, Glasgow

Magical Land

One day, there was a unicorn with a lovely, long tail that was all different colours like a rainbow. Ava, a girl, was walking along the park. She accidentally fell into the pond. When she fell into the water, she screamed for help. A magical horse appeared. She jumped on and started riding it through the water. Ava had never been on a unicorn before. She could see in front of her a magical forest with all different coloured rainbow unicorns. The horse took her far to the magical land of Rainbow Land and it was the best place ever.

Jenna Chi (8)
St Cuthbert's Primary School, Glasgow

Abbie Saves Magic Dog

One day, on Sugar Island, there was a magic unicorn called Abbie. She had a nice rainbow horn which dazzled. Abbie liked to play with everyone because she was friendly. Abbie loved animals because they are very fluffy and cute. Abbie would go back to Earth to save all the animals. Abbie arrived in Glasgow. She couldn't believe her eyes, there was a dog with a unicorn horn and it had dazzling glitter and it was a rainbow dog! Abbie picked the dog up and quickly ran away to a beautiful, magical place in Sugar Island.

Poppy Kelly (7)
St Cuthbert's Primary School, Glasgow

Robot Destruction

In the science lab, there was a scientist and a robot. But, one day, they were creating a portal and a magic potion. Suddenly, a hand appeared through the portal. The hand grabbed the scientist and pulled him in. The scientist was so strong, he broke the portal and he trapped the hand that appeared through the portal. The scientist started to take samples from the hand because he wanted to know where it came from. He wanted to see if it was an alien or a human hand. He wanted to find the rest of the body and blood.

Tyler Redmond (7)
St Cuthbert's Primary School, Glasgow

Bad Island

One day, there was a nice, beautiful, white unicorn called Katie. She had a sparkly rainbow horn. She lived in a magical place but there was a bad island where evil unicorns lived. Katie always wanted to go to the bad island to see what it was like. She wanted to see if she could turn bad unicorns good. She arrived at the bad island and met a bad unicorn. She was red and black and had a sharp, pointy horn. She looked at her and said, "I'm Thunderstorm, can we play?"
Katie said, "Can we be good best friends?"

Zoey Guan (7)
St Cuthbert's Primary School, Glasgow

Magic Magnet

One day, a girl named Katie slept in her big, pink bed. She woke up and rubbed her eyes. She shouted to her mum, "Mum, I'm going to the science centre!" She started to get ready. She put on black leggings and a purple top with a pink star. She brushed her long, blonde hair. Katie walked to school on her own. The bus was waiting to go on the trip. She arrived at the science centre. She saw a magic magnet. She wanted to touch it. It was glowing pink. She slowly touched it and she was dazzled.

April Newton Green (7)
St Cuthbert's Primary School, Glasgow

The Dark Night

A long, long time ago, there was a bad spy called Sam. Sam had a plan to rob the Queen. He wanted to steal the jewels and the Queen's crown. Since the spy was young, he wanted blue, sparkling jewels on the crown. His plan was to climb up a big, tall tree across from the palace and use a hook slide to fly across onto the roof of Buckingham Palace. He managed to get onto the roof but he did not know that the Queen had a device on the roof waiting for the spy ninja...

Patience Asemota (7)

St Cuthbert's Primary School, Glasgow

From Bad To Good!

As Lisa walked through Heroic Academy's doors, Star's, the head of the Supers, jaw dropped like a stone. She exclaimed, "Ladies and gentlemen, can I now present the good little witch!"

Lisa was so confused. *Boom! Crash!* A villain, well, Star's evil twin brother Scar, had come unexpectedly. All Mrs Star cared about was, "My nails, my hair! I only got them done this Tuesday!"

"Please calm down!" Lisa yelled. Just then, she lifted her hand and *kaboom!*

Scar stated, "Welcome to Heroic Academy!" Lisa noticed that she had done it, she'd turned him from bad to good!

Maya Mohamed (11)

Tany's Dell Primary School & Nursery, Harlow

Zong

It was a dark, stormy night in London. *Zoom! Boom! Crash!* A flying saucer hit the ground and out came an alien named Zong. He slithered down to Buckingham Palace. Zong quickly jumped down in the drains and climbed up the pipes. He ended up in the Queen's bed. He quickly slithered into the announcing room and said, "Me, Zong, king by killing Elizabeth!"

"What?" screeched Gareth. Gareth was a soldier, he ran into the announcing room and saw Zong and shouted, "Hey, stop!" Gareth shot his gun and made Zong disappear forever. "Phew!" Gareth said.

"I'll be back..."

Harrison Houghton (11)

Tany's Dell Primary School & Nursery, Harlow

Jessica And Pinky Blossom's Big Escape

As Jessica swung her axe for the last time, the last tree fell and sunlight burst through the canopy of the jungle. Sunlight filled the cave beneath and destroyed the tiger that had abducted her friend, Pinky Blossom. Jessica entered the cave to find her with a gobsmacked expression. "How did you ever find me?" she said. Jessica said it was the footprints in the mud, she recognised them from her survival training. "Can we get back to our game of hide-and-seek now?" asked Pinky Blossom.
"After that adventure, I'd rather play something less energetic!"
"Great idea, Jessica!"

Lara Burke (10)
Tany's Dell Primary School & Nursery, Harlow

Skyler And Amber

Skyler lives in foster care. Her parents died. She was ten. Skyler doesn't let people too close to her. She's scared to lose them. Amber broke that. Amber is the school singer. On Saturday, Amber visited Skyler to ask her help with homework. Skyler was singing in her bedroom. Amber went upstairs and was shocked. "You are amazing, please sing with me in the next Christmas production!" Skyler was shy.

Her foster mum said, "Please Skyler?"

Skyler said, "Yes!"

After practising daily, the big day came. The Christmas performance was marvellous. They received a school award.

Laura Lakatosova (10)

Tany's Dell Primary School & Nursery, Harlow

Blaise Granger And The Red Beryl Crystal

There was an enormous, castle-looking school with owls tweeting around the Grand Hall. Children gasped as the owls swooped down with their daily post. The lights were dim and the smell of candles filled the air.

"Welcome to Hogwarts!" bellowed a rather stern man named Professor Dumbledorin. There were two evil-looking teachers beside him. One of them was called Snase while the other Slyther. Suspiciously, Blaise Granger, Ronald Weasley and Henry Potter glanced over. They noticed that Snase was creeping off towards the Red Beryl Crystal guarded by the Phoenix. They rushed over and quickly took it slyly.

Perla Grigalaityte (11)
Tany's Dell Primary School & Nursery, Harlow

The Haunted Cabin

One cold and frosty night, two college students went to Camp Fun. The campers were led to their cabins.

Ten o'clock at night, the campers finished unpacking and went to bed. All of a sudden, one of the college students heard a really loud groan. Sophie, a girl from college, woke Kelly, another girl from college, up, shouting, "Kelly, wake up, I just heard a really loud groan!"

"No you didn't, you liar!" Then Sophie disappeared. Kelly couldn't believe it! She couldn't find Sophie anywhere. Kelly turned around because she heard a noise. There was a ghost. It was Sophie...

Tegan Rose Roberts (11)

Tany's Dell Primary School & Nursery, Harlow

Superhero Saves London

Boom! Bang! Suddenly a black figure appeared. He looked like an indestructible villain. Then another person came. He threw the villain into the boggy, green garbage bin. A group of villains came to try and attack this so-called superhero. The villain's friends then came to help him battle the mysterious superhero. Out of the blue, a whole group of superheroes came. They decided to fight. Whoever won got the city, London. One flew into a massive building. They charged at each other. The superheroes won the battle against the weird, annoying villains. There were no more attacks on London.

Jack Stone (10)
Tany's Dell Primary School & Nursery, Harlow

Binary

In 2208, people thought alternate universes didn't exist. One day, a rift opened in the sky and large ships full of grey, slender aliens glided through. Forty-two years later, the universe was devastated. Humans lived on a dead planet orbiting binary stars. The aliens had turned most of the 22,000,000,000 humans on Earth into mindless 'freaks'. Two brave commanders (Chambers and Oxford) set out to slay the head alien. They slashed and shot their way through the hordes of monsters they encountered. Commander Chambers brutally sliced the head alien in half, killing the aliens and saving the universe!

Alfie Chivrall (11)

Tany's Dell Primary School & Nursery, Harlow

The Door

Lillia attended a school for thieves called PAC (Practice and Capture). Her nickname was Shadow. She knew everything about her school except one thing. What was inside the white door? Shadow asked her friend, Jasmine, about the door. "You mean the white one?" she asked.
"Yes, I am sneaking in tonight!"
"Can I come?"
"Okay, see you at eight!" The friends met outside the door. They lockpicked their way inside. Inside was a beautiful red hat and coat. Jasmine did not have a costume yet, so she stole it and has used it ever since. Shadow also took some nunchucks.

Caitlin Moriarty (10)
Tany's Dell Primary School & Nursery, Harlow

What A Start To The Day

With solid-black spectacles, the shy detective started another day's work. Walking down the street, knowing he would be late, he took a shortcut. He walked timidly through the dark and spine-chilling forest, biting his nails. Without warning, a huge, eerie spider bounced from a hazel tree. The detective was terror-stricken. What a silly idea! From afar, he could see the elegance of an exquisite unicorn. Could this be! No detective on land had ever met a unicorn. He quickly befriended the beautiful beast, catching one last glimpse of the spider, they rode onto work. What a start to the day!

Iisha-Lemay Myers (10)

Tany's Dell Primary School & Nursery, Harlow

Mars

Finally, seven months had passed. Tomas and Niall Armstrong were on Mars. When they got to Mars, they set up camp and decided to sleep. Suddenly, something got Tomas and he disappeared. Niall decided to look for Tomas. All of a sudden, Niall fell in a hole. He found a room with aliens. He found Tomas stuck in a room. He hacked Tomas out with his super intergalactic teleporter. They got out and Tomas shouted, "They're going to destroy the world!" They told Earth, "Run and protect, aliens are coming!" All of a sudden, *boom!* Earth exploded. Earth was finished.

Kacper Zapior (10)
Tany's Dell Primary School & Nursery, Harlow

Royal Murder

There was a mystery going round town - a murder mystery involving the Royal Family. The rich royals were very friendly with a wealthy man named Richard. Even though the Royals had plenty of money (trillions) and a wonderful lifestyle, they wanted more. The Royal Family planned to kill Richard on the evening of Halloween. Dressed in masks and costumes, they snuck into Richard's house and stole all of his money. Unfortunately, they killed the wrong person - Richard's wife. They didn't realise that Richard had been in a costume watching them all along. Would they get away with it?

Teddy Cleverdon (10)

Tany's Dell Primary School & Nursery, Harlow

The Man Who Saved Us

Bang! Boom! The gunshots swept across the battlefield. Jeff was in the corner of the trench, then Sargeant Smith came along and shouted, "Get up you baby! We need all the men we can get!" Jeff jumped up and *bang!* The sniper shot flew to the French boss and killed him. Suddenly, a Breguet bomber plane flew over and bombed their trench, *bang!*

The next day, he found out that James, his friend, died. He travelled back home and cried for twenty days.

The next day, he went to the cemetery to pay his respects for James and was depressed.

Jake Carter (10)

Tany's Dell Primary School & Nursery, Harlow

Dino Land

Hello and welcome back to Jurassic Park. We have been exploring for a new species of dinos. Our sea divers have found a whale-like creature that is known as the Mosa but, scientifically, it is called the Mosasaurus. Our land explorers have found a dino too! For all that they know, it is fast, dangerous and it has no mercy. It is called the Utahraptor! Velociraptors are around eighteen feet long. The Utahraptor could easily be the biggest of the bunch! Our sky explorers have found a sky creature, the Quetzalcoatlus. It comes from North America! Thank you for listening!

Nicolas Gecmen (10)

Tany's Dell Primary School & Nursery, Harlow

The Case Cracker

"Right," said a guilty man who robbed a bank, killed everyone inside and blew it up, "I am getting so bored of these police exploring the ruins, my hand is getting tired killing them!" Then he thought of a sinister idea. Back at a block of flats was a man people called the Case Cracker.

"Guh!" he said while stuffing his face with doughnuts. "Who could this rat be? Those stupid police keep exploring the ruins and going missing! Probably dead now... Wherever the rat is, I am going to get him, no matter what happens to me..."

Oliver Quinn (10)
Tany's Dell Primary School & Nursery, Harlow

The Girl With Violet Hair

Once, there was a girl named Clementine with bluey-violet hair and green eyes. She was trapped on an island and was never allowed out unless the barrier was opened.

Until one magical day a prince named Ben (with brown, curly hair) thought it was not fair and opened the barrier to set her free. Clementine instantly fell in love with Ben and they spent long days together.

One day another girl stole a green-gemmed sceptre and the kingdom was in destruction. The clever prince put the sceptre back and saved all of his kingdom. They all lived happily ever after.

Isabelle Walker (11)

Tany's Dell Primary School & Nursery, Harlow

Larry Tudor

Larry Tudor was not a happy boy - he had a miserable time at school because he was bullied. However, one day, an exciting thing happened to him, he won a competition to go on a thrilling, exhilarating adventure to Coven's Castle for a whole year. After waving goodbye to his family, Larry was transported straight into the huge, ice-blue, sparkling castle. Larry learnt how to: make potions, make himself invisible and make people kinder. When Larry returned to his old school after a year, he was the most confident and likeable boy - Coven's Castle had worked its magic.

Archie Perks (11)
Tany's Dell Primary School & Nursery, Harlow

Christmas Spirit

In 1877, in a cold, dark alleyway, lived a young, small boy called Jim. One night, as Jim slept, a rich family called the Berkshires threw out their Christmas tree with the decorations. Not many things in Jim's life made him happy but Christmas did. So, he took it home. At midnight, while London lay silent, a wizard cast a spell on the tree and it came alive. Jim awoke from his slumber to the wonders going on above him. "Ho ho ho!" shouted a flying Santa decoration. Jim's heart sang. This year might actually be his best Christmas yet!

Oliver Berger (10)

Tany's Dell Primary School & Nursery, Harlow

The Tale Of Voltage

One stormy night in Velocity, during Halloween, a boy called Oakley was getting ready into his costume for trick or treating. Then, all of a sudden, the power went out. His mum was busy and thought it was just a coincidence. So, she asked Oakley to go and check it out. So, Oakley opened the circuit and then, *bang!* Oakley became Voltage. He didn't realise anything had changed so he went trick or treating. When he got back with his mates, he touched the doorknob and both his mates went flying. They were rushed to hospital and never seen again.

Cameron Bullock (11)
Tany's Dell Primary School & Nursery, Harlow

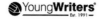

His Greatest Fear!

Boom! Kapow! It was the were-rabbit. Windows shattered as he thumped on the floor but he didn't want gold or diamonds. He wanted Cyborgamos Prime's iron stone, he wanted to use it to blow up the world. But then out from under the Brooklyn Bridge came Cyborgamos Prime with Ripply, who had the power to turn into anything in the universe. So he turned into a magma fireball and exploded onto the were-rabbit. He rolled, fell and died. The world was once again safe... but wait... they found an evil alien's egg! The end... or is it?

Alfie Hopkins (11)
Tany's Dell Primary School & Nursery, Harlow

Super Cat

One day, there was a boy called Odin. He had a dream of becoming a superhero. At school, he was doing amazing and, in maths, Odin would smash his tests, getting A+. His friends liked to play superheroes as well. One day, he was walking and fell. "Ouch!" Odin fell into radioactive water. When it was night-time and he went outside, he changed into his superhero form. One night, Odin unexcitedly said, "I wish there was crime!" Then he saw a villain. He jumped out of his window and stopped him. The police came and arrested him.

Archie Cleall (10)
Tany's Dell Primary School & Nursery, Harlow

Alien Attack!

I stepped through the rocket door, not knowing what I would find. When my eyes adjusted I saw an alien. The alien ran towards us shouting, "Fight!" Suddenly thousands of aliens charged forward.

Run, I thought. I just had to run quickly and escape. But they would not stop attacking. Then I pulled out a stinky sock I had in my pocket and they scrambled for their little lives.

Finally now I could do my job... Put the flag on the moon. I walked up and I proudly put the British flag where it should belong.

Niall Wright (10)

Tany's Dell Primary School & Nursery, Harlow

The Great Fight

One day, there were two brothers and they got into lots of fights. When they were walking together, they stumbled into a magic portal and it gave them powers. One was fire and one was water and it also gave them a weak spot. They went to the park to test out their powers and fire got hurt because water flooded fire.

The next week, fire came back and got revenge on water. Water was hurting everyone, so fire had to do something. Fire shot fire without water finding out and water had a slow, painful death. Now, everyone's safe.

Ronnie Wood (10)
Tany's Dell Primary School & Nursery, Harlow

Puggy Portal

Stepping through the black hole, I found myself on a faraway planet. I was really confused, then I realised there were only pugs staring at me, just as sceptical as I was. I looked deep into a cream pug's eyes until it suddenly collapsed. I saw flying cars with pugs in and pugs wearing necklaces. I knew I was in space when a pug floated over my head. There was a gorgeous goddess-looking pug in a flowy dress sitting on a golden throne. I was so shocked! It was absolutely berserk! In disbelief, I ran back through the puggy portal.

Siobhan David (10)

Tany's Dell Primary School & Nursery, Harlow

Hero School

Once upon a time, there was an extraordinary child and so the people who looked after her got her into hero school. She woke up with excitement. She raced to school. She didn't know anyone. She came into science class. Oops! She set her book on fire! She got detention. Someone else came in and sat near her. They talked but there was something mysterious about him. He took off his hood, his eyes were red! He blasted her with fire. She turned into a wolf and defeated him. He was actually a demon hiding under he could get her.

Lily-May Morton (10)
Tany's Dell Primary School & Nursery, Harlow

Who Got Murdered?

"Oh gosh! Argh! Someone is dead!"
One month later, the investigation started. Mrs Clifton, the investigator, had found some suspects, Mrs Della, Mrs Collinson and Mr Worton-Geer. They found out who died and it was a schoolgirl called Chloe but why would Mrs Della kill Chloe? They arrested her for first-degree murder. Mrs Della was let out for not killing Chloe, so she was off the hook. Chloe was shot in the head. They took Mr Worton-Geer to get evidence who knew Mrs Collinson killed all of the children that day! What!

Chloe Browne (10)
Tany's Dell Primary School & Nursery, Harlow

The Story Of Black Flames

One stormy night, a boy called Hero was playing out. He left his shoes outside and they got struck by lightning.

The next morning, he put them on his feet and then he fainted. He woke up and he felt different. He felt stronger. He went to his garden and ran to his trampoline. Something had changed. He was able to shoot lightning bolts and he had super speed.

For the next ten years, there was a battle against Red Flame. From that day on, they called him Black Flame. The battle came and he got hit in the chest.

Mikel Appleton (11)

Tany's Dell Primary School & Nursery, Harlow

Le Mans '66

Speeding along the race track, Ken Miles takes over another Ferrari in the Ford GT40 Mark II. We are two hours into the twenty-four hours of Le Mans and... oooh! #21 just crashed and is now in flames. Bruce McLaren just passed Farrarl and Farrarl does not look very happy with his drivers. Ken Miles has gone into the pits, looks like his brakes are busted. Only one minute left of Le Mans, who will win?

The race is over and Ford is first, second and third and this is history for Ford. Can they do it again next time?

Liam Willis (11)

Tany's Dell Primary School & Nursery, Harlow

The End

It was the end. The world was at war yet again. Cities in pieces as if they were Lego models. The Allies winning (just). Children crying as they saw their fathers going off to war. Mothers waving their children off on every platform of every station. But not Edward Jenkins. He did not have a family, like many children in 2508. But, one dreadful night, on Christmas Eve, he was shot. He was rushed to a hospital but died on the way. Just like that, another one dead. So, as I said, it was the end but also the beginning.

Max Peter Allen (11)
Tany's Dell Primary School & Nursery, Harlow

Time City Disaster

As the bomb was one hour from destruction, the bomber was about to leave but then Space Boy found the secret code to cancel the bomb. There was a black hole army defending the bomb cancellation unit. Space Boy had to battle the whole army just to get to the cancellation unit. Although he had a trick up his sleeve. He would bait them into jumping off the spire. But, then he realised he was missing a digit. The missing digit was in the forest. Eventually, he found it and managed to stop the bomb before it exploded.

James Forrest (11)
Tany's Dell Primary School & Nursery, Harlow

The Big Day

Dixie wiped her sweaty hands on her jeans and tuned her guitar until she was happy. She then strummed a tune and walked into the O2. This was the launch of her new album, Pink Over Purple, and she was very nervous. As the arena said her name, she knew it was time. She walked onto the stage and stared at the millions of fans. Suddenly, a fan grabbed her leg and pulled Dixie off the stage! Flashing lights and beeps were going fast. She woke up in a hospital bed. What had happened to her? Broken leg? Broken arm?

Rosie Barker (11)
Tany's Dell Primary School & Nursery, Harlow

Trapped In Hell

Once upon a time, there was a frog-humanoid who fell into Hell. She soon became the goddess of Hell but she still wanted to get out of there. She had been stuck down there for over ten years. She had a plan for escaping Hell. She followed everything on the map but one thing... She ended up against a demon so she got her scythe out and hit it. She knocked the demon out and carried on with her excellent plan. She found the hole to the Overworld. So, she used her climbing skills to get to the Overworld.

Brendon Dakin (10)
Tany's Dell Primary School & Nursery, Harlow

The Black Hole

I had a dream a couple of days ago. I felt like a balloon flying in the air. I saw the entire solar system from the window. The Earth and all of the planets around the sun looked like small tennis balls. In the distance, there was a big hole, the black hole, about to suck me in. I was spinning all around in the spaceship and it made me feel dizzy. After a couple of minutes, everything had stopped. I started waking up. I was screaming. For the first time in my life, I had a very alarming experience.

Gabriella Gora (10)
Tany's Dell Primary School & Nursery, Harlow

Haunted House

Once upon a time, there was a haunted house on top of a hill. Nobody lived there and it had been empty for fifty years. One cold October night, a boy called Timmy Smith thought he would find out of this was true. Timmy knocked on the front door. The door was slightly open. He was pulled into the house by a man. He was very scared.

A few hours later, he was left on his own in the room. Timmy decided to make a run for it and ran home without stopping. He never spoke about what happened.

Owen Ellis Halls (10)

Tany's Dell Primary School & Nursery, Harlow

The Boy And The Time Machine

Once upon a time in 2031, there was a boy. He worked on a farm and, one day, he found a huge, metal telephone box. The young boy said to his sister, "Hey, I found something!" The girl quickly ran. The girl was shocked.
She said, "OMG! That is a time machine!" The boy was shocked. They got in and went to the future. They were in 4056. Thye just got out and a truck took their time machine. They didn't know. They turned around and, on the truck, there was a label. It was in Area 51...

Kamil Zapior (10)
Tany's Dell Primary School & Nursery, Harlow

The Mystery Of The Boy And The UFO

There was a boy roaming the gloomy, dull streets of London called Zack. He was on the way back from playing with his friends. He was all alone and he was not too sure of his way back, so he picked up his phone and tried to call his auntie, but his phone was dead. He panicked and then turned around a corner that led to a dead end. Then, out of the corner of his eye, he saw something peculiar, it was like a UFO! He then realised there were two of them! He went to investigate...

Jayden O'Reilly (10)
Tany's Dell Primary School & Nursery, Harlow

Alien Attack

Once, there was an alien and he wanted to invade the world. So, then, he went and was destroying the world. So, I came and went to save the world. I went and there were fires and buildings burning, not good. But, I was going to save the world. Don't worry! I was to the rescue. I went in and stopped him and put him in prison, then I had a party. I invited everyone and did a roast. I was so happy! We danced and everything but, anyway, bye! We are gonna have fun.

Tegan Elizabeth Hodgson (10)
Tany's Dell Primary School & Nursery, Harlow

The Adventures Of Waffle Man

Waffle Man heard a noise. He turned to find Toaster had crept up on him. A scuffle broke out, lots of screaming was heard. They rolled around the kitchen, grappling. Waffle Man kicked Toaster but Toaster moved away too quick. Toaster grabbed Waffle Man by the waist. Suddenly, everything went black. Bob was woken up by a burning smell. It was Waffle Man, he was being toasted. Bob ate him.

Una Venezia Turner-Porter (10)

Tany's Dell Primary School & Nursery, Harlow

Detective Albert

The last battle began. It was 1890, the scene was set in the dark, closed, creaky museum. On top of the T-rex's ancient dinosaur bones stood brave Detective Albert. His green hat shone in the light like a diamond. His green cloak hung around him like Batman's. On the T-rex's head stood Evil Foxy, waiting for Detective Albert to speak. "Halt in the name of the law!" shouted Detective Albert.
Evil Foxy attacked Detective Albert who quickly used his magic flying walking stick against Foxy. Evil Foxy tripped and all the bones fell. Detective Albert was rescued by his stick!

Albert Lock (10)
The Forest School, Knaresborough

The Jzmlolz

Once upon a time, the city was okay. Suddenly, an electric ball hit. The ball went over the entire city. It went black. Two years later, Jack was running across the fixed city. Jack noticed a new train had been built. Jack went on the train, a white and red monorail. An aeroplane hit the train! Jack went flying. Jack hit the floor with a bang. Albert was there. Albert had some weird creatures. Jack said, "What are they?"
Albert said, "They are monsters."
Jack, Albert and the monsters formed a team to defeat Doctor Desenaror.

Jack
The Forest School, Knaresborough

Anna And Nieve's Adventure

Anna the beautiful unicorn and Nieve were best friends at The Forest School. One day, they were eating chicken dinner with stuffing, carrots, broccoli and chocolate cake with custard for pudding. At the end of the day, Anna's ice portal opened for her to go home. Nieve went with Anna through the portal for a sleepover. Anna lived in a big, blue castle. Anna and Nieve talked about their good day and made rainbow slime. At four o'clock in the morning, Anna and Nieve went to sleep and were snoring. The next day, Nieve and Anna rode their bikes.

Nieve Mountford (10)

The Forest School, Knaresborough

Zack The Scary Demon

One day, there was a little boy called Zack. He was frightened of everything. His brother made him jump all the time. One day, Zack ran away and found a mansion. It looked horrendous but went in. Zack got cursed! Then, he turned into a demon and he wasn't scared anymore. Actually, everyone was frightened of him! Zack felt happy and he scared everyone all day and all night. Zack felt cheerful at first, but then he got bored and went back into the mansion. Zack looked at the full moon and the curse lifted. Zack was never scared again.

Leo Hill (10)

The Forest School, Knaresborough

The Hunt

The secret agent was on a mission to hunt the car thief. He was speeding and he was disintegrating people. The climate was changing, it was getting colder. He needed shelter, so he went into a building for the night. The secret agent was losing hope but then he saw him in the distance - Evil Edgar. He ran swiftly to Edgar. Evil Edgar ran away quickly. The secret agent ran faster. Evil Edgar fell to the ground, he went to prison and was never seen again. He got prison food on Christmas Day and coal for a Christmas present.

William Whitehead
The Forest School, Knaresborough

The Midnight Sky

The sky was full of stars and moons when Moonlight the magic wolf flew across the sky. She saw a magic portal and stepped through it, not knowing what was on the other side. A hideous dragon came and swooped Moonlight up and took her to the land of dragons! Moonlight was so terrified, she turned invisible, so the dragons couldn't see her. She saw herself again and the dragons saw her and she was so scared. She flew back into the sky to her underground lair where she stayed and waited. She was safe at last.

Sophie

The Forest School, Knaresborough

The Hidden

One day, I was walking down Woodville Terrace and I saw the woods. I walked through the forest. It was very dark. Then, I saw an abandoned hospital. My cousin went missing in that hospital when a bomb went off, so I went in. I turned on my flashlight and saw a figure run past. There was a loose floorboard with a door handle on it. I pulled on it and it opened. I went under. It was a graveyard! I found my cousin Charlie and he had been hiding from dangerous wolves!

Conner
The Forest School, Knaresborough

YoungWriters® Est. 1991

YOUNG WRITERS
INFORMATION

We hope you have enjoyed reading this book – and that you will continue to in the coming years.

If you're a young writer who enjoys reading and creative writing, or the parent of an enthusiastic poet or story writer, do visit our website **www.youngwriters.co.uk**. Here you will find free competitions, workshops and games, as well as recommended reads, a poetry glossary and our blog. There's lots to keep budding writers motivated to write!

If you would like to order further copies of this book, or any of our other titles, then please give us a call or order via your online account.

Young Writers
Remus House
Coltsfoot Drive
Peterborough
PE2 9BF
(01733) 890066
info@youngwriters.co.uk

Join in the conversation!
Tips, news, giveaways and much more!

 **YoungWritersUK**   **@YoungWritersCW**